Jack
and the
Beanstalk

and me!

For Charles, Samuel and Emilia — E.B.

First published 2015 by Nosy Crow Ltd
The Crow's Nest, 10a Lant Street
London SE1 1QR
www.nosycrow.com
ISBN 978 0 85763 472 6 (HB)
ISBN 978 0 85763 473 3 (PB)
Nosy Crow and associated logos are trademarks
and/or registered trademarks of Nosy Crow Ltd
Text © Nosy Crow 2015
Illustrations © Nosy Crow 2014
The right of Ed Bryan to be identified as the
illustrator of this work has been asserted.

A CIP catalogue record for this book is available from the British Library.
Printed in China
Papers used by Nosy Crow are made from wood grown in
sustainable forests.
1 3 5 7 9 8 6 4 2 (HB)
1 3 5 7 9 8 6 4 2 (PB)

Jack
and the
Beanstalk

 nosy crow

Illustrated by
Ed Bryan

Once upon a time, there was a boy called **Jack** who lived with his mother in a tiny little cottage. They were **very** poor.

Jack was a good boy, and he was very brave, but he didn't always think things through.

One day, Jack's mother asked her son to take their COW to the market. "We have nothing to eat and no money," she said. "We have to sell Daisy."

Jack **fed** Daisy, **cleaned** her
and put a **bell** around her neck,
then he set off for the market.

Jack and Daisy had not gone very far before they met a strange-looking man with an old **suitcase.**

"Hello, young man," said the stranger. "What a **lovely cow** you've got! If you give her to me, you can have ten of these **magic beans.**"

"How **exciting!**" Jack replied. "I'll take them!"

But when Jack got home and showed his mother the beans, she was **very** angry.

"I can't believe you swapped our **only cow** for these ridiculous **beans!**" she shouted.

"But they're **magic beans!**" Jack cried.
"They're not magic, you **silly** boy!" said his mum,
and she threw the beans out of the window.

The very next morning, when Jack woke up, he found an **enormous** beanstalk in his garden. He decided to climb to the very top!

Jack climbed **higher** and **higher** and **higher.**

The beanstalk seemed to go on **forever!**

At last, Jack reached the **top** of the beanstalk. To his amazement, a long path led to a **huge castle** in the clouds!

Jack walked up to the castle doors and went inside.

Straight away, a little mouse ran up to Jack. "This is the **giant's** castle," it said. "He's **scary!**"

"I'm **not** afraid of giants!" said Jack. "I'm going to have a look around."

The first room Jack found was the **kitchen**, where a **cook** was making soup. "**Please**, can you help me?" said the cook. "The giant wants his **lunch!**"

Jack chopped the vegetables and stirred the ingredients. Soon the soup smelled delicious.

"Oh, thank you," said the cook. "Because you've helped me, I'll tell you where the giant keeps his stolen gold."

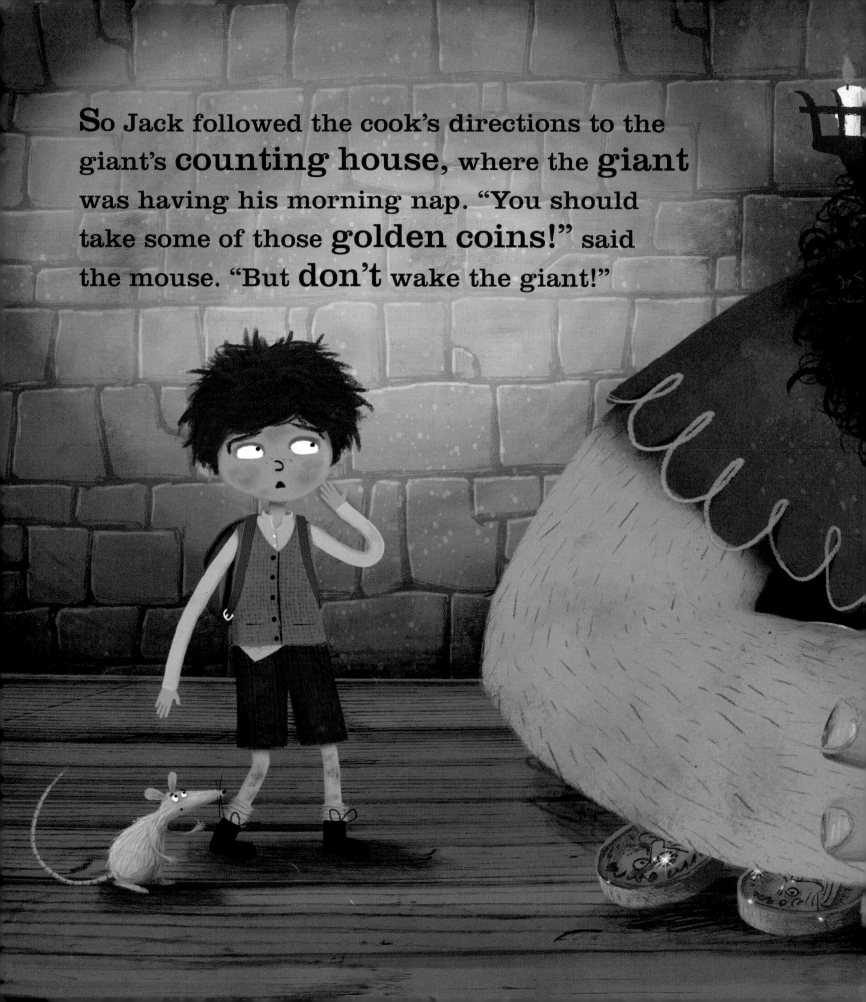

So Jack followed the cook's directions to the giant's **counting house**, where the **giant** was having his morning nap. "You should take some of those **golden coins!**" said the mouse. "But **don't** wake the giant!"

Jack **carefully** lifted the giant's hands and took the **coins.** He stuffed them into his bag then crept out of the room.

Jack kept exploring. Soon he found a room where a **frog** sat by a **well.**

"**Please**, can you help me?" said the frog. "The giant stole my **golden ball** and threw it down this well!"

Jack lowered the **bucket** into the well, scooped up
the ball and wound the bucket up again.
The frog **hopped** for joy.

"**Oh, thank you,**" said the frog.
"Because you've helped me, I'll tell you where
the giant keeps his stolen **magic goose.**"

So Jack went to the **goosery**, where the **giant** was sleeping after his lunch.

"One of these geese lays **golden eggs**," said the mouse, "but which one? Whatever you do, **don't** wake the giant!"

Jack lifted each goose, one after the other, until he found a **golden egg!** He tucked the egg and the goose into his bag, then crept out of the room.

Underneath the castle, Jack found the dungeon,
where a baby dragon was locked up in a cell.
"Please, can you help me?" said the dragon.
"I'm just a baby and I want to go home to my mum!"

Jack took the **big iron key** off its hook on the wall,
turned it in the lock and **freed** the baby dragon.

"**Oh, thank you,**" said the dragon.
"Because you've helped me, I'll tell you where
the giant keeps his stolen **golden harp.**"

Happy Honky Tonk ltd

So Jack made his way to the music room where the giant was having another nap! "Please, can you help me?" said a little golden harp. "I want to escape from the giant. He's so mean."

Jack picked up the harp, but it suddenly started to shout.

"I tricked you!" it screeched.
"I'm going to call my master now!

Master Giant,
wakey wakey!
This boy Jack is trying
to take me!"

The giant woke up and glared around him.
"Fee, fi, fo, fum," he boomed.
"I can smell you! Here I come!"

The giant **chased** Jack
through the castle.

"You may think that you're
the **winner**, but I'll eat you up
for **dinner!**" shouted the giant.

The giant **chased** Jack down the beanstalk.

"You can try to **run away,** but I'll eat you up **today!**" the giant yelled.

When Jack reached the ground, he grabbed an **axe** and chopped the beanstalk down. It toppled over with a loud **CRASH!**

The giant was **never** seen or heard of again. And as for Jack and his mother, they both lived **happily** ever after.